OUTSIDE

SANDRA R. ANDERSSON

ISBN: 978-91-88385-12-3

1

"I don't like porridge tablets," Lee complained. She didn't mean to sound so whiny; the words just came out that way.

A brief shadow of concern passed over Liesl's face, but the almost constant smile was quickly restored. "Eat them anyway, dear," she said and patted her daughter's hand. "They're good for you."

"But they taste like ... nothing at all," said Lee and put the small beige tablet back in its wrapping.

"You don't eat something for the taste, silly," said Kate who had come into the open-plan area of their small accommodation unit where they did everything besides sleeping. "You eat to stay healthy and productive. Food provides the nutrients your body requires to be able to function as a good citizen and accumulate learning during a long day at school."

Lee had heard it all before, both from her mothers and from the preceptors in kindergarten and school. Individually prepared food tablets made sure that the earth's resources weren't wasted or unevenly distributed.

Kate continued the lecture. "They contain everything your body needs, exactly when you need it. So I don't want to hear any more whining from you." Despite her strict words, she gave Lee an affectionate pat on the cheek. "Eat the breakfast that has been prepared especially for you and be grateful that you don't ever have to know what it feels like to suffer from starvation or malnutrition."

"Yes, Mom." Lee sighed, picked the tablet out of the wrapper again and put it on her tongue where it immediately started to dissolve. Her mother was right, as usual. There was so much to be grateful for. It was unproductive and bad for morale to wish for something more when all her bodily needs were constantly met. She would have to discuss these feelings with her counselor at their next session.

Lee took her glass over to the dispensing unit in the wall, put the glass in the small compartment, shut the protective plastic door and pressed the inside of her wrist against the small scanner next to it. Just once she wished that the dispenser would dispense something other than water.

It could dispense anything at all; she knew that. Her mothers got a dark brown coffee-flavored beverage in the mornings and a dark red beverage on Friday nights that smelled weird, although they seemed to enjoy it. Babies and toddlers got formula, specifically adapted for their age segment. The preschoolers could get milk or water, depending on their individual needs, but for children over the age of seven the dispenser always served up water.

What she would give for some variation. That the glass would contain a pink or green fluid when she took the glass out. Blue, perhaps.

She couldn't even begin to imagine what a blue fluid would taste like. It didn't even have to taste like anything other than water. Nothing much, anyway. Just something ... different.

The door to the compartment opened, and Lee took her glass and looked down into it, expectantly. Water. Of course. She took a big gulp and swallowed down the faint aftertaste of the porridge pill. Then she stared at the water, left in her glass. Dull, transparent water, tasting of nothing at all. Same as yesterday, same as tomorrow. She glanced over her shoulder. Her mothers were busy, not looking her way. Quickly, Lee poured the water into the pot of the large fern in the corner. She put her glass in the wall unit to clean and sterilize it for next time. There, breakfast was over.

Time for school.

Just as she was leaving, the screen on the wall in the living room came on, and a green community logo started swirling over the dark screen. There was a light melodious sound coming from hidden speakers all over the accommodation unit and both Kate and Liesl came and stood alongside Lee in front of the screen.

The logo disappeared, and a communications channel opened up. A woman was sitting behind a desk in a very tidy office. She had a data screen next to her that she was reading from until she noticed that the channel had opened.

"Oh, there you are. Good morning," she said and adjusted her immaculate hair.

"Good morning," the entire family replied in a chorus.

"My name is Genny Fisher, from the Reproductive and Placement Services. I'm pleased to inform you that your household has been assigned a new family member." The woman scrolled through the data that appeared to be floating in the air just to the right of her. "Congratulations, you have a brand new daughter. She will be delivered to your accommodation unit sometime tomorrow. All necessary equipment will be included in the shipment."

Kate gasped and grabbed hold of Liesl's arm. Liesl just stared at the screen. "Oh, thank you," she mumbled. "Thank you so much for choosing us ... We had no idea that we were even under consideration ... It's been so long ..." She grabbed Lee and pulled her in front of her, facing the screen. "Lee here is ten, already."

Lee pulled herself away from her mother's strong grip. Liesl turned toward Kate, and they fell into each other's arms. "We're going to have a baby!" Liesl squealed, and Kate just laughed and hugged her. "A brand new baby!" Kate turned toward the screen. "Oh, excuse me, what is she called?"

The woman scrolled through the green glowing data once more. "Let me see ... This child seems to not have been assigned a name yet. I'm sure that information will be included in the shipment. If that particular data is not part of the package, you can ask one of your family's counselors to check the records at the next session."

"Oh, thank you, again," gushed Liesl. Lee didn't think she had ever seen her this happy. Kate was also radiant with joy, but Lee wasn't entirely sure what she thought about the news. A new baby sister. Oh, she had wanted a sister, so very much, when she was younger. But now, at ten, what was she going to do with a baby? It would be years and years before that baby could do anything other than poop and sleep. By that time, Lee would be all grown up and at work all day. What was the point of a sister then?

"I have to go to school," she said, but her mothers didn't hear a word she said. They were busy crying and laughing and hugging. Lee slipped out the door. The temperature outside more or less matched the one inside of their small accommodation unit, but she still shivered while she waited for the school shuttle down on the corner.

2

The driverless shuttle dropped Lee off outside the school building. It looked pretty much exactly the same as the house where she lived, except for the small plaque beside the door that declared it to be Educational Facility I:46. Lee and the other children passed through the doors into the hallway and up the stairs to the classrooms. Jennily caught up with Lee on the stairs and tapped her on the shoulder.

"Morning," she said brightly.

Lee didn't know why it bothered her. Most people were always smiling. There was no reason not to. But over the last couple of days Lee hadn't been in the mood for smiling, and the call this morning had left her with a strange sensation somewhere inside the belt on her pale blue jumpsuit. She couldn't put her finger on it, but something was not quite right.

"Morning," Lee replied.

Jennily started blabbing about their homework, something about assignment 4D that she had gotten completely wrong, but Lee wasn't listening. She was trying to locate the feeling that had been bothering her, but she wasn't sure exactly how to do that. She supposed that she could ask Helenifer, but her next session with the counselor wasn't until Saturday. And she wasn't sure how she was even going to explain this to Helenifer. There wasn't anything wrong. Everything was exactly the way it always was, exactly the way it had always been. Everything was always just fine.

So why did she feel like she wanted to kick something?

"You're not listening!" Jennily exclaimed, and that bright smile was replaced by a discontent frown.

Lee looked at her friend. That was weird. She had never seen Jennily so upset. "I'm sorry. I guess I'm a bit distracted this morning. I just found out I'm getting a new sister."

Jennily raised her eyebrows. "A new sister? You're excused. That's major news. Are the parental units excited or are they also walking around with a look of 'whu-what?' on their faces?"

Lee smiled. "They're thrilled. Of course. Why wouldn't they be?"

"Exactly," said Jennily giving Lee one last stern look before dropping her off outside of her classroom. "Babies are the cutest. Not as cute as me, but still. You're going to love being an older sister. But please don't ignore me. That's all I'm saying. See you at lunch?"

Lee raised her hand and started to walk into the classroom. "Definitely. And I'm sorry. It won't happen again."

"Oh, I'm sure it will," Jennily said grumpily and started walking toward her own classroom.

Lee went to find her seat. She leaned back in her chair and put on the headset. The goggles and headphones shut out all sights and sounds that weren't immediately relevant to the work she was about to do. Lee could hear her preceptor greeting them all and noticed her feedback on last week's assignment up in the right corner of her field of vision. Lee quickly looked through the correct solutions to the problems and compared them to her own answers – satisfactory, according to her preceptor's notes – before she swiped everything to the side and focused on her preceptor's morning speech. It was always inspirational and motivating and usually made Lee feel committed and enthusiastic, but today the words felt empty and hollow. Meaningless.

Lee shut out her preceptor's monotonous voice and started scrolling through this week's schedule. There were several new assignments. She could never decide whether it was better to start with the fun stuff or if she ought to save those for last. She decided to alternate this week. Boring history first and then some math. She didn't think she would have time for more than that today. The history assignment looked like it would take a lot of time.

She activated the history assignment and suddenly her schedule and preceptor were gone. The classroom had disappeared, and it looked as if she was standing in the central square of the pod. It wasn't significantly different to the way it looked today, but the buildings were not as gleaming and the people didn't wear light blue jumpsuits. A voice started to narrate the scenes, and Lee realized that it was not her pod she was looking at. Oh, yeah, her preceptor might have mentioned that there had been other pods, many, many years ago, but the others had perished so very long ago that the information hadn't seemed relevant somehow. Still, it was a useful lesson, Lee figured. It was important to remember what had gone wrong for all the other domes, so it didn't happen here as well. They had to learn from those other women's mistakes if they weren't to repeat them.

Lee tried to concentrate on the sights and sounds of ancient Greece. Where was that now? As soon as she had thought that, a translucent map appeared in the corner of her eye. Oh, all the way over there, on the other side of the world. But even though these people had lived in such a different place, they still looked pretty much like Lee and her family and friends. Dark, straight hair. Light brown skin, brown eyes that looked a bit slanted due to the epicanthic fold of the upper eyelid. Not very tall, but slim, with narrow hips.

Lee studied the scene in front of her, the birthplace of democracy. She guessed she was supposed to think that this was important, but Lee found it difficult to muster any interest in the women standing there at the Acropolis, wearing something that looked like white bed sheets wrapped around their pale green jump-suits. She just didn't feel connected to them, living so far away in such a different world, many thousands of years ago. And their ideas felt so alien, so completely unrealistic. Well, it was easy for her to think that when she knew how it had ended. Their entire dome had per-ished, as had all the others, because of their strange ideas about individual freedom and liberties.

It felt good living in a different time when they knew better. Lee knew her role in the pod had been decided the moment she was conceived in one of the Department of Reproductive and Placement Services laboratories. The job she was going to perform had already been chosen for her and would be waiting when she had finished her training and become tall enough to work the machines at whatever plant she was assigned to. It would all be revealed on her thirteenth birthday, and it was nice and comforting to know that her part in the pod's future was already taken care of. Every decision had already been made. She was needed and therefore she had been created. Everyone had to do their duty, fulfill their purpose and stick to the plan. Otherwise, the entire pod was in danger.

No, history was not for her. She was more interested in the future. But if history was so much like now, she didn't suppose that there was much hope for something different in the future. A different color jumpsuit, maybe, in a few hundred years. Big deal.

A new sister. Perhaps that was as exciting as the future got around here.

Lee would rather have had something blue to drink.

3

As soon as Lee entered the crowded lunchroom, she heard Jennily's contagious laughter.

"So," Lee said, sitting down on the bench next to her friend. "Have you forgiven me, then?"

Jennily took another sip from her large glass of water and smiled at her as if she didn't have a care in the world. "Forgiven you? What are you talking about?"

Lee breathed a sigh of relief. Whatever had bothered Jennily earlier seemed to have passed, and her mood was back to bright and sunny.

"Nothing," said Lee and smiled back. "Have you had your lunch already?"

Jennily got up and followed her over to the dispensers. "No, just some water. What are you in the mood for today?"

Lee looked at the dispenser door and tried to picture what might be inside the small compartment when the doors opened. "I don't know," she said, but something made her keep her thoughts from this morning to herself. Jennily would think she was mad. But if she couldn't have something blue to drink, perhaps she could have something red to eat? Something red and cold that tickled her tongue. She laughed at the thought and held up her wrist to the scanner. There was a rattle inside the dispenser, and the doors opened. A small packet with two pills inside. "Oh," she said and tried to not sound disappointed. "Pizza again. That's what I got yesterday and the day before."

"That's strange," said Jennily and scanned her wrist at the dispenser next to Lee's. "We never get the same food two days in a row. Not even the same week, I don't think. But this week, I've been getting the same meals two or three times." She picked up her own small packet and turned it over. "Tikka masala. That's nice. I haven't had that for a while. That's Indian food, you know. Have you studied India yet?"

Lee shook her head. "No. I had Greece today, though. In history."

Jennily nodded. "I've done that already. I thought it was very interesting. And I loved the togas they wore over their jumpsuits. I tried to make one, but my moms didn't like it when I played with the bed linen."

Lee laughed. "No, I don't think mine would be too pleased with that either."

Jennily tore open her packet, popped her pills in the back of her mouth and swallowed them down whole with a big gulp of water. "Ok, I'm done. Do you want to go outside before we head back to class?"

Lee put her pizza tablets on her tongue and felt them starting to dissolve. The faint flavor was pleasant enough, but not as appealing on the third day in a row. She nodded at her friend. "Sure. I have some time left on my break."

When she saw the line to the drink dispenser, Lee decided to skip her lunch beverage. She would rather go outside than spend her entire break standing in line. She was feeling a bit thirsty, but knowing that it would only be water again made her ignore the sensation. Instead, they walked outside and sat on the ground with their backs against the wall.

Jennily leaned her head back and tilted her face up against the dome. "It's nice today. I can almost feel the sun."

Lee leaned back as well and looked up at the semitransparent cover that shielded the inhabitants of the dome from the elements. "Yes. I love summer."

Even though there wasn't much difference between the seasons, she still liked it when the dome was lit up like this and glowing in the sun, instead of gray and dull and streaming with rain or sleet. Inside the dome, the temperature was more or less constant, and pretty much the same inside the buildings and out, but there were subtle differences. Lee tried to imagine what it would be like to live without a dome over her head. If the sun could shine directly on her face and the rain could pour down over her head. She shook her head slowly. Now, this was something that Helenifer would like Lee to tell her about so she could explain to her why this was impossible. But suddenly, Lee felt an intense urge to keep the feelings from the last couple of days from her teacher. She didn't have much that was her own, but she did have her thoughts. And however disturbing and unusual they were, she would like to keep them.

4

When Lee returned from school, the accommodation unit was quiet and empty. She sat down
in front of the large screen on the wall and activated the sofa table keyboard with the inside of
her wrist. The screen lit up, and she could see
her homework assignments. Only two, today.
That shouldn't take too long.

But Lee was still struggling with her last
math problem when Liesl came in through the
door with a wide smile on her face.

"Hello darling!" she gushed and hurried over
to give Lee a quick hug.

"Hi, Mom." Lee frowned at the screen.

Liesl started babbling on about how everyone at work had been so excited to hear about the new baby and Lee lost her train of thought. Just as she was about to figure out why her calculations didn't add up! She turned toward her mother and glared at her.

"Mom, I'm trying to do my homework!"

Liesl looked surprised. "Oh, I'm sorry, dear. But there's really no need to sound so cross. Should I call Helenifer and ask if she has time for a quick session, to try and figure out what's wrong?"

Lee felt the annoyance from earlier beginning to spread through her entire body. Why did it always have to be like that? Why must every feeling be poked and prodded and analyzed to pieces, until she didn't feel much of anything anymore? Helenifer was great at her job; she was the best counselor Lee had ever had, but she was always placating, always soothing. And right now, that was not what Lee wanted. She didn't want to calm down, take a deep breath and smile at everyone. She wanted to rant and rage and scream.

The thought startled her with its intensity. Where had that come from? She wasn't usually like this. Lee shook her head and tried to smile at her mother.

"No, Mom. There's no need. I'll speak to her on Saturday. I'm fine."

Liesl came over to the sofa and looked at the homework on the screen. "Have you been working on this since you came back from school?" she said, noting the digits at the lower left edge of the display. "You have! It says here that you've been active for more than three hours! Lee, really! What have I told you about taking breaks?" Her mother looked concerned and reached out to stroke the hair out of Lee's face.

Lee looked at the screen. "I ... didn't realize that it had been so long. This math problem ..."

"But then you haven't even had your dinner, sweetheart," Liesl continued. "You should have eaten more than an hour ago. No wonder you look so tired. Honestly, Lee, do I need to get Mrs. Swindon to come and sit with you after school? Because if we can't rely on you to care for yourself, then we will have to ..."

"No!" said Lee sharply. She quickly adjusted the tone of her voice. "No," she repeated, more calmly. "There's no need for Mrs. Swindon. I'm fine. I just forgot, that's all."

Liesl looked worried but eventually she smiled at her daughter. "All right then. Hurry up and get your dinner. Your mom will be here soon, and then we could watch some tv, if you like?"

Lee closed down her homework and walked over to the dispenser on the wall. "No, thanks," she said and scanned her wrist. The dispenser rattled, and she took her glass and put it in the small compartment while she tore open the packet of pills. Pizza again? Something was not right. "I think I'll go in my room and read a little." She took her glass out of the dispenser, not even bothering to check the contents this time. What was the point?

Her room was small, not much more than a narrow cubicle with a bed on the wall above her desk and storage units hidden away under the steps leading up to the bed. But it was the only room in their accommodation unit that had a small window, and that's where Lee was headed. She sat down on the steps halfway up to her bed and leaned her head against the wall. The building where they lived was almost at the edge of their pod, and if Lee sat on the right step, she could see a large slice of the dome between the two buildings across the street. At this time of night, the protective cover was glowing with the setting sun, and Lee sat there, sipping her water, looking at the yellowish golden glow until it slowly melted away and turned into darkness. The something that had been bothering her also melted away, a little more for every sip of water that she took. When the glass was empty, she could no longer remember what it had felt like.

5

Sometime during the night, there was a commotion outside. Lee emerged from her heavy sleep to hear voices and engines and vehicles. She turned over in her bed and noticed a flashing orange glow on the ceiling of her small room. She drowsily climbed down a couple of steps and peeked outside. The street behind her building was filled with people in sturdy jumpsuits and hardhats. A truck with a crane was unloading some sort of scaffolding, and somewhere behind the buildings across the street, a strange light was coming from a wide dark splotch along the curvature of the dome.

Lee stared at the unfamiliar sheen. It was a bluish white, intense light, completely different from the distorted sunlight that she was used to under the dome. It took a while before her drowsy mind realized what it was she was looking at.

The moon.

It was full and looked massive and heavy and almost within reach, there just above the treetops.

Treetops! Lee sat up and rubbed her eyes. The dome had been breached. A wide crack reached from above the roofs of the buildings behind the one where she lived, all the way down to the ground, where a myriad of maintenance workers and vehicles had gathered. Through the rift, the trees outside were almost black against the night sky, but there was something about their razor-sharp contours against the heaven above that was so completely different from the usual blur caused by the semi-transparent dome. So that was what trees really looked like.

There wasn't much to see in the dark, but Lee sat at her small window staring out into the darkness for as long as she could stay awake.

When the sun came up and woke her again, the rift in the dome had been concealed behind a huge scaffolding, almost taller than the buildings next to it. It was still very early. A glance at the screen over her desk told her that she should have slept for another hour and a half and if she had been safely tucked away in her comfortable bed instead of sitting awkwardly on the hard stairs she probably would have.

The street outside was empty, and the scaffolding did its best to look inconspicuous and not draw attention to itself. There was not a glimpse of the trees or the sky outside to be seen. Lee stared at the thick tarpaulin and noticed a small movement at the bottom, to the left. Was there someone there? She fixed her eyes and searched for the shape of one of the maintenance workers, or perhaps some kind of supervisor, but couldn't see anyone. Then she stared at the scaffolding again, measuring it with her eyes. It was enormous. Amazing that they had managed to erect that huge structure overnight, without anyone noticing the commotion.

But she had heard it. She had woken. She had seen the moon in the sky over the treetops. Not much of a glimpse of the Outside, but more than anyone she knew had ever gotten. If only it hadn't happened in the middle of the night; then she could have gone closer and seen more before they covered up the rift ... Had the maintenance workers managed to seal the dome already? Probably not. That must be what the scaffolding was for, after all. To keep all the dangers of the Outside out of the dome. To keep all the women in the dome safe. To keep them from seeing the sky, the moon, perhaps even the sun rising ...

Her heart started beating faster at the thought of getting a glimpse of the sky again, in daylight. Before she knew what she was doing, she slipped down the stairs, found her jumpsuit and quickly pulled it on. She ought to go back to bed. That would be the right thing to do. Go back to bed and get the rest of the sleep she needed to perform to the best of her ability in her classes later today. She knew that. And she intended to go back to bed. But before she did, she needed to see ...

The door to her mothers' room was closed, and Lee hurried toward the front door. In the hallway, the lights were dimmed, just like in the accommodation unit, but she had no trouble seeing where she was going. She hurried down the stairs and out the front door.

There was no one around when she more or less ran around the side of the building to the street behind it. She crossed the street and then slowed down, looking around her, listening for movement behind the tarpaulin. The lower left corner was still moving, a slow, rhythmic motion that she now realized wasn't caused by a person. But what was it caused by?

She walked slowly toward the tarpaulin with her heart in her throat. The edges were over-lapping, and the outer sheet lifted and fell back down toward the inner, over and over. Lee swallowed, felt the dryness in her mouth and throat and wished that she had grabbed a glass of water before she had left the accommodation unit. Then she shook her head. Any minute now, those workers might come back to start repairing the dome. She just had to see what it was like, Outside, before that happened. Just a peek.

She steeled herself, lifted a trembling hand and grabbed hold of the outer layer of tarpaulin. The flapping motion stopped when she pulled the tarp toward her, but then something hit her in the face, and she gasped and dropped the heavy fabric.

Something cold and ... What was that? She rubbed her face with a trembling hand. There didn't seem to be any damage, except that her eyes felt uncomfortably dry, but it went away after a few blinks. She glanced over her shoulder, back at the house where she lived. She shouldn't be here. Perhaps it would be better if she returned to the accommodation unit, drank a glass of water and went back to bed for another hour.

Then she looked at the flapping tarpaulin and sighed. Yes, it would be the right thing to do. But then she would never know.

The curiosity spurred her on, and she got another, sturdier, grip on the tarpaulin and pulled it aside. There it was again.

Something cold but invisible stroking her face.

Lee felt chills all the way down her back but didn't drop the tarpaulin this time. Instead, she blinked repeatedly to counteract the dryness of her eyes and slipped in under the scaffolding.

Inside the tarp-covered scaffolding, the light was different. Glowing, golden, almost magic. It was coming from a tall rift in the dull semi-transparent dome. Lee could actually see the rays of light slanting in between the jagged edges. It was colder here, but she kept moving toward the light. That cold thing kept hitting her face, and she could feel it against the rest of the body too. It was so strange, like the air itself was moving, of its own volition. She had never felt anything like it.

Lee came up to the opening, squinting against the intense dawn sunlight. She raised her hand to shield her eyes and peeked out.

Almost immediately, her legs gave way, and she sat down on the ground, gasping for air. Air that felt cold and sharp and crisp and stronger than what she was used to, somehow. Her head was spinning, and her eyes couldn't seem to focus. The Outside was so huge, so bright, so cold, so colorful, so different ... So much more than she could ever have imagined.

6

Her eyes slowly adjusted to the bright sunlight and she tried to stand up. Her knees were trembling, but she grabbed one of the poles supporting the scaffolding and managed to get back on her feet.

Instead of looking at the sky that was so impossibly high above the dome, she kept her eyes firmly glued to the ground and focused on one small thing at a time. The bright green grass that grew unkempt up to her knees. The huge tree that lay just outside the opening, with broken branches and the top part severed by a huge saw. It must have been the tree that broke the dome. It was enormous, as tall as her house, and even when it was lying flat on the ground, it was so tall she could barely see over it. The bark was dry and brittle, more gray than brown, and some of the branches didn't have any leaves on them.

After a while, her legs stopped trembling, and she straightened her back, slowly raising her eyes to look at the trees, the ones that were still standing. They were impossibly tall and now that her eyes had adjusted to the new, strange light, she realized that they actually moved a little from side to side. At first, she thought it was just the fact that her eyes weren't used to seeing things so far away, but then she thought that perhaps it had something to do with the fact that the air was moving. Looking at it made her a bit dizzy. They were too big to be moving like that!

Something else that was strange and overwhelming was the sounds. There was a rustling and a whooshing and some sort of smattering and something melodic that she couldn't understand and seemed to be coming from all directions at once so that she didn't have a chance of pinpointing the source. Some of the sounds were sharp and hurt her ears. Others softer and more varied in a manner that was quite pleasing, once she got used to it. The crisp and cool air felt the same way, giving her a headache and tickling her nose at first, but after a while, she started noticing different scents, both pleasant and not so nice.

Despite the alienness of the outside world, she couldn't help taking a step through the opening and out onto the soft, thick grass. Only for a minute or so. She just wanted to see a little more, perhaps touch a few things. Find out what was making that tweeting noise that seemed to be coming from over by the trees. It wouldn't take long. But the memories would last her a lifetime.

It was difficult to walk on the uneven ground, and her soft slippers didn't quite shield her feet against the hard tree branches and rocks that she stepped on. On sore feet, she slowly made her way around the large tree trunk, grabbing hold of protruding branches for balance, in order to see what was on the other side.

More grass, some bushes and in tufts here and there were small but colorful flowers. Yellow and blue and pinkish purple. Lee stared at them, moving slowly back and forth with the air. She fell on her knees in front of one of the tufts and just smiled at the colorful petals. It looked as if they were nodding their small heads at her in greeting.

"Hello," she whispered and jumped at the unfamiliar sound of her own voice in this alien environment. She quickly looked around her, but of course, she was alone. No one had heard her.

She sat there, in the soft grass with her back against the enormous tree trunk, feeling the sun on her face and slowly exploring the Outside with her eyes. It was magnificent, in all its intimidating, overwhelming hugeness. The shapes and structures were so unusual, and the scale of things made her dizzy. All those sounds that she couldn't identify ought to make her tremble with fear, but instead, they just made her feel really warm and calm inside.

Once she had gotten over the initial shock of being outside, she was happy that she had seized this opportunity. She knew that this was a unique, once-in-a-lifetime experience, one that other girls never got to experience, and she memorized as many of the details as she could, to bring with her the memories, at least. Still, it would be difficult to go back inside and see her familiar surroundings. What would the dome look like, compared with her new experiences?

Just as she was getting up from the grass to go back, she heard a sound that made her skin crawl. It came from inside the dome. Voices. Oh no. She crouched behind the tree trunk and peeked over toward the opening. Suddenly the scaffolding was a hive of activity; there were workers everywhere, in thick, sturdy jumpsuits, gloves and a transparent, airtight cover over their hard hats, with a filter of some sort in front of their mouths. Of course, they would need protection while they were working so close to this hazardous environment. She could hear them speaking and laughing, their voices muffled by the protective gear, and the clanging noise their tools made against the metal poles as they climbed up to higher levels.

Oh no. She had stayed outside too long. How was she going to get back in again, with all those people there? She tried to look for an opportunity, a small gap when everyone was busy elsewhere, but there were so many of them, and someone was always right by the opening for some reason.

She struggled to make out what they were saying. "Several days' work," someone said. "Complicated repairs," said a woman on the second tier. "At least we don't have to work around the clock," said someone else further up. Lee rubbed her face and tried to think while an unfamiliar sense of worry spread through her slightly chilled body. Too late. She had left it too late. Only a couple of minutes, that had been the plan. And what was she supposed to do now? She would never be able to get back in through the gap with all those people there. They would see her, inevitably, and then what? She couldn't even imagine what the consequences might be. Nothing like this had ever happened before.

If it was going to take the workers several days to fix the opening, and they weren't going to work all hours, then Lee might be able to get back in tonight.

But that would mean that she'd have to spend the entire day out here. She glanced over her shoulder at the dark trees standing tall behind her. Could she do that? Was it possible to survive an entire day out here, in the Outside? Without all the protective gear that the maintenance workers were wearing? Without food or water?

Well, it was just for one day. She had never gone without food before but didn't think that one day would be enough for that starvation thing that Kate was always going on about. It would be uncomfortable. The most difficult thing she had ever done. But the more she thought about it, the more she became convinced that she could do it. She had experienced thirst before, several times over the last few days actually, since she had been so fed up with that water. It was unpleasant but not impossible to endure for a short period of time.

The workers would surely not work past six. What could that be, twelve hours or so? But she couldn't sit here for twelve hours straight. She was already feeling cold and thirsty, and it was still early in the morning. She would have to move further away from here. If she just sat here, she risked being seen by one of the maintenance workers. She would freeze if she stayed still and as soon as she got up, someone might notice the movement.

She tried not to think about all the dangers, out here. About all the reasons that womankind had built the domes in the first place. Radiation. Pollution. Famine. Flooding. Sure, those were horrible things, and millions of women had died. But those pre-historic women, thousands of years ago, had lived Outside all the time. They hadn't had a safe dome to return to at nightfall. Lee shivered and rubbed her arms. She could do it. She was a slightly above average student and had shown reasonable problem-solving skills in school on several occasions. She glanced at the tree line, at the intimidating shapes, rising toward the sky, dark and foreboding. This was just another problem for her to solve. If she applied all she had learned in school about being meticulous, careful, thorough and cautious, she could surely do this.

She turned around and took one last look at the crack in the dome, the dull sheen of the surface glowing in the morning sun. When every-one in sight was busy with their backs turned, she got up on unsteady legs and hurried toward the tree line. Twelve hours. She would just have to survive until nightfall.

7

Lee made it to the tree line with only a couple of stumbles. There were so many things to trip over, but the fear of being caught where she was not allowed to be kept her on her feet. Soon she was concealed by the semi-darkness between the tall trees. She stopped, half-hidden by a massive tree trunk and looked back at the dome. The activity inside the rift seemed to be taking place mostly at the top end. They must be working from the top down. That was good. That meant that she would have no problem getting back in, as soon as they had stopped working tonight.

No, the problem she had to figure out a solution to was how she was going to survive out here, for twelve hours or more, with no food or water and no clue about what fears lie awaiting her behind these trees.

The tree line had looked so massive, like a wall of tree trunks, but once she had stepped into the forest, it was actually both light and airy, and she could see the golden dawn sunlight slanting down toward the ground here and there through gaps in the canopy. The ground was soft and covered in something brown and brittle that crackled when she walked. It took a while before she recognized the shapes of the leaves on the trees and matched them to the shapes on the ground before her. She was walking on old leaves! The few trees that grew inside the dome also shed their leaves in the fall, but the leaves were always removed promptly. Out here, there was no one to clean up the mess. There was no one at all.

The realization that she was completely alone in the entire Outside made her stop and grab a thick tree branch for support. As far as she knew, she was the first person to ever set foot among these trees. No one ever left the dome. It was not possible to live out here, she knew that of course, that was the whole point, but the Outside world hadn't seemed as severe as she had expected. The air was thick and difficult to breathe, but now that she had gotten used to it, it smelled fresh and not at all toxic. The ground was uneven and tricky to move across, but as long as she paid attention and looked where she was going, she would be fine. She just needed to find a safe place, not too far from the dome, somewhere sheltered from this constantly moving air, where she could sit in the sun. The shade under the trees was dappled and looked pretty, but she was beginning to get cold. Her blue jumpsuit was too thin and flimsy to protect her from the moving air, and her bare arms were covered in small bumps that seemed to be temperature related and not some kind of reaction to the toxic surroundings as she had first thought.

Her stomach felt hollow, and once again she wished that she had grabbed her breakfast before sneaking out. How on earth was she going to manage twelve hours or more? She had always had regular meals, every day of her life, and she had no idea how her body would react to a prolonged fast. Judging by the rumblings from her stomach, not too well. Her tongue was dry and fuzzy. What she wouldn't give for a glass of water.

She saw a lighter patch a bit further along and walked toward it. It was a small clearing among the trees, a rather steep hill down toward a meandering stream. Lee hesitated before venturing out into the open, but the warmth of the sun pulled her out from the shadows, and she sat down on the grass and slid carefully down the slope.

It took a while before she recognized it as water. It bore no resemblance to the fluid that came out of the dispensing units in the accommodation unit or in school. It moved across the stony creek bed in twists and jumps, and the sound it made was unlike anything she had ever heard. Lee slowly approached the stream and fell on her knees right beside it. One hand reached out to touch it and came back wet. She smelled the water and then tried it with the tip of her tongue. It didn't taste bad, just strange. She dipped her hand again and licked it. It was water. If only she had a glass. She leaned down and let the flowing water stream across her tongue. The stream shifted and splashed her in the face, and she sat up and gasped for air.

The water was so cold, and there was so much of it, but still she had such difficulties getting something to drink. She tried again, this time pushing some of the water toward her face and noticed that she could shape her hand so that some of the water stayed in the palm of her hand long enough for her to drink it. It wasn't much, but she did it again and again until her stomach didn't feel so empty anymore.

Lee found a dip in the grassy bank, where she curled up and rubbed her arms. The small bumps seemed to be receding, slightly. She closed her eyes and turned her face to the sun. The warmth on her cheeks spread slowly throughout her entire body, and she started to relax. This wasn't so bad. Everything was going to be all right. She could do this. Just for one day. It would be the adventure of a lifetime. A story she could tell her granddaughters one day. Not that they would believe a word of it. Lee smiled, snuggled against the soft grass and lay there listening to all the unfamiliar sounds and the water over the rocks. The tensions and fears of the unknown surroundings slowly faded, and after a while, she dozed off.

A shrill sound woke her suddenly a couple of hours later, and Lee sat up, staring left and right. The frightening noise echoed in her ears, but it wasn't repeated, and she curled up in her small hollow again, scanning her surroundings for whatever could have made that sound.

It was warmer now, with the sun high in the sky, and Lee felt a strange burning sensation on the right side of her face. When she put her hand there, the skin felt hot and tender to the touch. She let her hands wander over her body in search of other symptoms, but couldn't find anything specific.

Her stomach felt hollow again, and she was just about to sneak back for some more water when she noticed a movement a little further up the stream. She pulled back, trying to stay out of sight. She stared at the tree line on the other side of the creek and saw something moving toward the water. It was some kind of animal, not even knee high, covered in reddish fur from the pointy nose to the long tail in the back. It had beady black eyes and looked suspiciously from side to side as it advanced toward the water.

Lee could hardly breathe. The hollow she was in didn't offer much in the way of protection, so she slowly inched her way back up the slope toward the tree line. She stepped into the shadows behind a massive tree trunk, grabbed the tree and clung to it, her heart pounding. What was that creature? And what would it do to her, if it saw her? She stayed completely still and— just like the animal—kept looking from side to side to try and discover any other dangers before they discovered her.

It felt like an eternity, but was perhaps only a few minutes or so, before yet another danger appeared.

8

It came along the stream, from her right, moving slowly but purposefully. Unlike the first creature, this one wasn't covered in fur. And unlike the first creature, this one walked on two legs, just like Lee. But it was no woman. It was taller than a woman, maybe one or two heads taller than either of her mothers, and its skin was pale, not soft light brown like hers. The hair on its head was light, almost gleaming in the sun, surrounding what was obviously the head in soft, loose curls. It had two eyes, a nose, and a mouth, just like a woman, but its features were exaggerated. The nose was bigger and more prominent, and its chin was strong and jutted forward in a way Lee had never seen before.

When the creature noticed the other creature further up along the stream, it stopped, almost precisely at the spot where Lee had been sitting earlier. She clung to her tree trunk and stared at it. It seemed to hunch down and sat on its haunches, studying the other animal. What would happen now? What happened when two creatures met in the Outside? Did they fight? Kill each other? Lee almost didn't dare to look, but at the same time, she couldn't take her eyes off them. The tall, two-legged creature pulled something off its back, and Lee leaned closer to try and see what it was doing.

It seemed to be some kind of container for carrying things around in, because the creature pulled on a zipper and opened the container wide. It pulled out something in a plastic wrapper. Lee could hear the crinkle that reminded her of the wrappers surrounding her food tablets. The sound made her stomach growl again, settled by the water but not at all content with it. Lee wrapped her arms around her to try and shield the sound from escaping and pulled back further out of sight, but the creature didn't seem to have noticed the noise. It pulled something out of the plastic wrapper, placed it on the ground and then retreated back the way it had come.

Lee peered out from the darkness, trying to make out what it was. It was too far down the slope to see clearly, but it looked brown, like the leaves on the ground, and a bit crumbly. It was in several pieces, and the inside of it looked lighter than the outside. She had no idea what it was or why the creature would have left it there on the ground by the stream, but then she noticed a movement in the corner of her eye.

The furry creature was coming closer, with its pointy nose in the air. It looked as if it was smelling something, but when Lee raised her own small nose and sniffed, she couldn't detect anything apart from the same strong forest smells that had bombarded her since she left the dome. The creature slowly approached the brown crumbly things that the tall figure had left behind. It stopped several times, sniffing and looking around from side to side. Eventually, it made it all the way to whatever was on the ground. Lee held her breath when the animal bent down over it ... and started to eat it!

Lee couldn't help but gasp. She didn't understand anything about what was going on in front of her, but the hunger in her recognized the same urge in another being. What was that? And what was it eating? Her growling stomach wondered if she might be able to eat it too, but her brain rejected the thought as being completely unreasonable.

She moved around to the other side of the tree to get a better view of the other creature. It had pulled back a bit and sat on its haunches behind an outcrop that probably shielded it from the furry creature's sight, but Lee could see it quite clearly from her vantage point at the top of the slope.

The more she looked at it, the more she became convinced that it wasn't an animal, even though she had never seen a woman who looked anything like that. But what else could it be? Women were the only creatures on earth that walked around on two legs and wore clothes. The creature's tall and gangly body was covered in something that bore no resemblance to her own blue jumpsuit but was definitely some kind of clothing. It seemed to be in two parts, where the top was red and had letters on the front— she could make out a U and perhaps a C, but there were more—and the bottom part was kind of blue, but uneven, so that there were lighter patches around what she called the knees and darker along the sides where there was a thin line for some reason that Lee couldn't see. The being stared at the furry creature. Then it pulled something out of the carrying container and pointed it at the beast that was finishing off the last of the crumbly pieces.

Lee stared at the thing in the being's hand— squarish, with rounded corners, pale green with some silver details that glinted in the sunlight— and then at the unsuspecting furry creature that had backed up a little and was licking its mouth with a surprisingly pink tongue. What was that two-legged being trying to do? Was it trying to capture it somehow? Or perhaps kill it?

She vaguely remembered something she had heard in a history assignment a long time ago; that the reason for the domes was because the Outside was so savage, and there had been a lot of aggression and killing in pre-historic times, before people came to live Inside. She had no idea if this being was planning to kill the four-legged creature, but the perfectly normal act of eating had made the furry little face look a lot less menacing, and she no longer felt that the small creature was any threat to her. That two-legged thing, though. She couldn't let it kill a perfectly innocent little furry thing. She just couldn't.

Lee flew out from her hiding place and ran down the slope.

"No," she shouted and waved her arms. "Don't kill it! Don't!"

9

The furry creature took one look at the running girl and disappeared into the forest on the other side of the stream so fast that it looked like a thin red streak against the browns and greens of its surroundings. Lee slowed down and steered away from the two-legged creature that had gotten up from its hiding place. It was staring at her, and it looked quite angry.

"Why did you do that for?" it said, in a perfectly normal voice, only a bit darker than Lee was used to. "I was just about to get a great shot, and now you've ruined it."

Lee gasped and stared at the strange being that was so obviously a person, just like her, only so completely different in every way that her brain couldn't make any sense of it. "I couldn't let you kill it!" she said and hoped that the being wouldn't point its shooting thing at her instead, now that its first prey had gotten away.

The being raised its eyebrows, and its forehead crinkled just like mommy Kate's used to do sometimes. "Kill it?" it said, and the disgusted frown made it obvious that Lee might have gotten the wrong end of the stick. "I wasn't going to ... I would never ..." It held up the shooting thing, and Lee staggered backward, raising her arms to shield herself. "I just wanted to take a photo of it."

Lee stumbled on a tuft of grass and landed undignified on her bottom, still staring at the being. "A ... photo?" she said and stared at the squarish green thing in the being's hand. It might still be dangerous, but she wasn't dead yet, so perhaps ... "What is that?"

The being straightened its back and stared at her, its eyes wandering over her from head to toe as if seeing her for the first time. "Wait a minute ..." it said. "Who are you?"

Lee sat up and tried to not show her fear. "I'm Lee," she said and crossed her arms. "So who are you?"

The being looked at her jumpsuit. "You're one of them ..." it said and turned and looked over the trees behind Lee.

Lee got up from the ground and turned to follow the two-legged being's stare. The top of the dome poked up over the tree line. "Of course I am," she said annoyed. "Who else would I be? There is no one else. We're the only ones on the planet. So the question is, who are you? Or rather *what* are you? You don't look like any girl I've ever seen."

The frown vanished, and the being's face lit up with a wide smile. "That's because I'm not," it said. "My name is Hardy. And I'm a boy."

10

Lee stared at the being. The word meant nothing to her. "A what?"

The boy's smile faded a bit. "You know. A boy. The other kind."

Lee shook her head, trying to clear some of the confusion. "The other kind of what?"

The smile had now completely vanished. "Are you kidding me? Do you seriously not know what a boy is? What do you think your dad was when he was little?"

Lee felt like her skull was starting to shrink. There was an aching across her forehead, from side to side. "What is a dad?" she whispered.

The boy frowned again. He looked at her piercingly, as if trying to determine if she was being serious. "You know. Moms and dads. That's where babies come from."

"Babies come from the Reproductive and Placement Services," Lee whispered. "I'm getting a baby sister today. They called yesterday with the news. Both of my moms are really excited."

She clung to this, the facts as she knew them. This ... boy creature must come from a different kind of dome, where things worked differently. Except there weren't any other domes. Not anymore. She had always been told that theirs was the only one left. Why would the preceptors say such a thing, if it weren't true?

The boy shrugged. "Sure, it's different when you have two moms," he said. "Or two dads. I know a guy with two dads."

Lee kept staring at the boy creature. It looked remarkably like her, and at the same time so very different. The tone of its skin was several shades lighter, but the irises in its eyes were the same shade of brown as hers, so dark that she almost couldn't tell where the iris ended and the pupil began. The eyes were the only familiar feature, but they looked weird in that pale face. Still, she recognized the confusion in them as matching her own. She was not the only one who didn't know everything. That was a consolation.

"So ..." she said and tried to wrap her brain around these new concepts. "In your dome ... there are both moms and ... dads?"

The boy laughed. "I don't live in a dome," he said. "I live in a town, a couple of miles that way." He jerked his head backward and slightly to the left.

Lee's eyes narrowed. "What is a town? And how can you live without a dome? It's not possible to live in the Outside."

The boy, Hardy, smiled. "Oh yeah? And why is that?"

"Because of the radiation from the sun, and the toxins in the air, and the weather. The Outside is too harsh for womankind. That's why our foremothers built the dome. And that's why we never go Outside."

The boy glanced up at the sun. "The sun is what keeps us all alive," he said and took a deep breath. "And does this air smell toxic to you? Not to me. And as for the weather, sure, it can get quite fierce during winter, but then we just stay inside more. In our houses."

Lee felt the confusion starting to creep up on her again. "So you live in a house? With your ... dad? In the Outside?"

"With my mom and my dad. And my brother, Ferdo."

Lee frowned again. "What is a brother?"

The boy smiled. "Like a sister, only it's a boy."

Lee couldn't make head nor tails of this conversation. "So, are there only ... boys in your dom— I mean, town?"

The boy shook his head. "No, of course not. It's just that in my family, there are only boys. I don't have a sister."

"And are all boys ..." She wanted to reach out and feel the pale skin on his arm, to find out if it felt the same as hers, but didn't dare. "... the same as you?"

"The same as me, how?"

She held out her light brown arm next to his several shades lighter. "The same … paleness."

The boy laughed. "Pretty much. Just like the girls."

Lee frowned. "But all girls look like me."

Hardy shook his head. "No, they don't. Here, let me show you." He pulled out the shooting thing from his pocket and Lee stepped back but he didn't point it at her this time. Instead, he dragged his finger across the top and touched the shiny front in a couple of different places. Then he turned it toward her so that she could see. "Here are some pictures of my classmates, when we went to the amusement park last week. See? These are boys here," he pointed at some of the small faces that appeared on the screen when he tilted the shooting thing from side to side. "And these here are girls. Lucitte, Karinda, and Joselle. I think Karinda has some Asian ancestors because you remind me of her, but she is also really white."

Lee stared at the screen. The girl's eyes had the same shape as her own but where disturbingly blue and the rest of the face was as pale as Hardy's. "Asian? What is Asian?"

Hardy shrugged. "Someone whose ancestors lived in Asia."

Lee shook her head. "My foremothers have lived here, always," she whispered. "Is this Asia?"

Hardy smiled. "No, this is Oregon, USA. Your ancestors must have been moved here in the ..."

He stopped abruptly and looked as if he regretted having said that.

"In the what?" Lee insisted. The things he said didn't make any sense, but she still didn't want him to stop talking.

"In the Doming," Hardy whispered.

11

Hardy stared at her as if seeing her for the first time. "You need to go back. Come on; I'll take you."

"Wait! What does it mean?" Lee urged him. It was obvious that he knew things, unbelievable things, things about her, even, and it felt unfair, like he had an advantage, having heard of her kind when she had never heard of … boys or whatever they were called.

Judging by the images on the small screen of his shooting thing, there were both boys and girls in the Outside, and they appeared to be more varied in appearance than the women in her dome. Even though the Outsiders were mostly pale, like this Hardy, some were taller, and others were shorter. One of the girls on the small screen had darker hair that looked almost red. What if there were beings in the Outside, in all shapes and colors? Lee felt stupid and small, like she had been kept in the dark all her life, while everyone else had been allowed to be outside and play in the sun.

Hardy looked as if he didn't want to tell her, but eventually, he did. "What we were taught in school was that the domes were built in the early 21st century because humans were in danger of becoming extinct. There were just too many people in the world that didn't get along and they didn't manage the earth's resources in a responsible manner. They threw garbage everywhere, even in the water, and they cut down so many trees that there were almost none left. People were selfish and violent. If they wanted something that wasn't theirs, they would just take it. Many, many people were killed for no reason. They used to have something called democracy—"

"Oh, I've heard of that," Lee interrupted him. "In Greece."

Hardy looked surprised. "So you know all this?"

"They believed that everyone should make the decisions together," Lee said. "It didn't work. That's why their dome became extinct."

Hardy frowned. "Yeah ... Except that there weren't any domes. Not in ancient Greece."

Lee blushed. "That's what I was taught in school," she mumbled.

"But you're right about the part that it didn't work," Hardy continued. "Everyone had a vote, and they were supposed to use that vote to make the best decisions for everyone, except they didn't. They kept making the wrong decisions, and things just got worse and worse."

Lee stared at him. "So what happened?"

Hardy shrugged. "The Decision Makers took charge."

"Who?"

"I don't know much about them, no one knows, but they built the domes—"

"There were seven domes, to begin with," said Lee confidently. This part of history she remembered. "One for each of the continents. But all the others are extinct now."

"No. I think there are about a thousand, in all. And I've never heard about any dome becoming extinct."

Lee felt dizzy. She had just about been able to picture another six domes, spread over the planet. But a thousand? Who lived in those other domes? And did all of them believe that they lived in the only one? That they were the only people left on the planet? "But … how …?"

Hardy shook his head. "I didn't pay much attention during this class, I'm sorry. I just didn't feel that it was something that I would ever need to know. But as far as I recall, the domes contain housing for millions of people. They were designed so that as many people as possible would be able to live on as little land as possible. The domes are closed systems with no negative environmental impact on their sur-roundings and maximum efficiency when it comes to food production and waste manage-ment—"

"That is correct," Lee interrupted. "Every-thing in the dome is very efficient. Efficiency is one of the pillars of our society."

Hardy looked surprised. "What are the others?"

Lee recited them without hesitation. She had learned them by heart when she was little. "The pillars of our community are Efficiency, Duty, and Harmony," she said. "Everyone must do their duty—efficiently and without waste—and we must all do our utmost to get along. Differences of opinion lead to friction which leads to violence which leads to destruction."

Hardy shook his head. "Okay ..." he said. "Anyway, the democracy-thing didn't work because the majority of people didn't understand the consequences of their choices. The Doming was a drastic measure, but it was for their own good. Someone had to take charge. The Decision Makers saved the human race from extinction. If most of the people lived inside of domes, it would quickly reverse the effect of many generations of pollution and over-consumption. After only a hundred years, the earth would be restored and ..." Hardy stopped talking and looked down.

Lee had never felt so stupid in her entire life. How come she had never questioned any of the things she had been told? She thought back to her history lesson yesterday. Those women in Greece with their togas and silly ideas about democracy. If the things Hardy told her were true, then all of that had been a lie. The women on the other side of the planet hadn't lived in a dome. Perhaps they hadn't looked just like her either. They might not even have been wearing those stupid togas over their jumpsuits. And there would have been dads there, as well. And what had he called them ... brothers. It was all so difficult to wrap her brain around.

Then she remembered something Hardy had said. "After a hundred years, what?" she said. "What would happen then?"

Hardy was still looking down at the ground, as if there was something very interesting going on in the grass in front of his feet. "Well, they said it would take a hundred years for the environment to heal itself, but then ... I don't know what was supposed to happen then."

Lee leaned forward to see his face. "What do you mean, what was supposed to happen? How long ago was the Doming? Are the hundred years up soon? Will we be moving back into the Outside?" The thought both thrilled and scared her. She started counting backward in her head. "Wait. My grandmothers were born in the dome. And they told me stories about their mothers and grandmothers, growing up in the dome. No one has ever mentioned anything about living Outside, not since our foremothers built the domes, thousands and thousands of years ago … I think that is something they might have mentioned," she said pointedly. "Are you absolutely sure you've got that right?"

Hardy glanced at her. "The Doming was … more than seven hundred years ago."

Lee frowned. "I don't understand. You said …"

Hardy shrugged a little and looked embarrassed. "I don't know. I'm sorry. I guess I thought that the people living in the domes were going to be there forever. It's not something people talk about, but whenever I asked my dad, he would say that they … That you were happy there and didn't want to leave." He glanced over at the dome again. "But if what you say is true, that no one knows or remembers ..."

Lee followed his stare. The dome gleamed dully in the sun that was high in the sky by now. "You mean, I could have lived in the Outside, all my life? And my mothers, and their mothers?"

Hardy shook his head. "I don't know what the plan was. I've never thought about it, okay? Which is embarrassing, considering my dad is a programmer ..."

"What's a programmer?"

Hardy looked down. "The programmers run the computer systems inside the dome."

Lee stared at him. "Your dad knows about the domes? How they work?" She looked back at the dome. "Does he know why we live there? Still? Why they haven't let us out?"

Hardy looked shocked. "Let you out? It's not as if you're locked in!"

Lee raised her eyebrows. "Are you kidding me? It's exactly as if we're locked in. Only worse. Because I never even knew that I was locked in. I never even considered the possibility of living anywhere else. All my life I've been told that no one can survive in the Outside. That there is no life on earth, besides the women and girls in our dome. If you believe those things to be true, why would you ever want to go Outside? But now, you're telling me that there are other domes … Thousands of other domes. And that there are boys and dads and girls with skin in different colors and hair that look like … I don't know what to think. I don't understand." She fell on her knees in the soft grass, taking deep breaths of the clean, scented air. It hardly felt strange anymore. How quickly she had gotten used to that.

"Come on," Hardy said and bent down. "Get up. You need to get back. You shouldn't be out here. You need to go back to where you belong."

Lee stared up at him. "I can't. Not now. I have to stay Outside until tonight, when they stop working on the repairs." She turned and looked over toward the dome. "But how can I go back now? What would I tell my mothers? That every-thing is a lie? That there are other women in other domes? That there are other beings, men and boys? They will never believe me. They will think that I've been broken somehow, by being in the Outside." She rubbed her face with her hands and looked pleadingly at Hardy. "What am I going to do now?"

"What is there to do?" Hardy said, and she thought that he sounded worried. "You go back inside the dome, of course you do. To your mothers. Don't you miss them?" he urged, but she just shook her head.

"What does that mean? Miss?"

He shrugged. "You know, that feeling you get when someone you love goes away?"

Lee just looked at him. "No one ever goes away," she said slowly. "No one ever goes anywhere. Everyone is always ... there."

He reached down and grabbed her by the arm to help her up. "Good. Then that's where you should be too."

She let herself be pulled up on her feet, but when he started to move toward the dome, she didn't follow him.

"Come on, we have to go," he said, pleadingly.

But Lee just shook her head. "I can't. Not now. And not until I find out more about this. You said that your dad knows about the domes. Can I meet him?"

Hardy frowned. "What ... You mean, come back to my place?"

Lee felt a shiver through her entire body. "Yes."

12

It was obvious that Hardy didn't think it was a good idea, but in the end, he sighed and started walking along the stream in the direction he had come from. Lee followed him. They walked along the stream until it parted in two, then continued along the left branch, mostly down-hill. Lee tried to take in all the new sights and the varied landscape but had to concentrate on Hardy's back and the uneven ground that he moved so effortlessly over. It was still difficult to walk, but she thought she might eventually get the hang of it.

When Hardy stopped to drink some of the flowing water in the stream, Lee turned and looked back the way they had come. The dome was no longer visible above the tree line. A moment of panic seized her. How would she ever get back Inside? But then the uneasy feelings returned. Did she even want to? And besides, Hardy knew the way.

They continued walking for a little while longer and eventually came to a gate in a fence. It was about as tall as Hardy, but the gate opened easily without even scanning his wrist. Stepping through the gate, Lee was hit once again with the realization that she was in a place where she was not supposed to be, doing something she was not supposed to do. This was not her duty. She wrapped her arms around her and followed Hardy through the opening.

On the other side of the fence, there was no forest, and Lee stopped and stared at the open, well-kept and landscaped park. There were trees, here and there, but most of it was just one big smooth lawn. Lee stepped carefully onto it and felt her foot sink down into the soft grass. Hardy had just kept walking, and she hurried to catch up to him. It was easier walking on this grass, almost like the ground inside the dome. She could see structures further ahead and felt an uneasy feeling in her stomach.

Hardy slowed down, staring at the buildings and then turning toward her, sweeping with his concerned stare from her straight black hair all the way down her pale blue jumpsuit. "You can't go into town looking like that," he said. "They'll know you're one of them ..." He took his carrying container from his shoulder and unzipped the opening again. He pulled out something gray and soft, balled up in a bundle, and held it out to her. "Here. Put this on."

Lee stared at it, but reached out her hand and took it. It folded out and revealed sleeves, just like a jumpsuit, and a zipper in front, like she was used to. But it appeared to only cover the top part of her body, even though it was much too big. She pulled it on and closed the zipper. The fabric was soft and smooth, thicker than the materials of her jumpsuit and not as crinkly. Hardy stepped forward and grabbed some leftover fabric at the back of her neck. "Here, put the hood up. And tuck your hair in."

Lee reached for it, but couldn't figure out what to do with it. Instead, she let Hardy pull the fabric up over her head. It covered her hair while leaving the face free, an unfamiliar sensation but not uncomfortable, and when she had tucked her black hair under it, Hardy nodded. "That will have to do," he said. "Now, we're going into town. My house isn't far, but if we meet someone, I don't want you to say anything to them, okay? Just smile and nod if they say anything."

Lee's eyes widened but she nodded and pulled the too-long sleeves down over her hands.

She followed Hardy over the lawn and onto a narrow street, winding slightly uphill. The structures on both sides of the street bore no resemblance to the buildings in her dome, and not even to each other, being of different shapes, sizes, and colors. There was so much space surrounding them, mostly smooth, soft lawn like the one they crossed to get into town. Most of the lawns were surrounded by low fences or walls, but they didn't seem to serve any purpose. Lee could have stepped right over most of them, without any real effort.

Hardy stopped at the gate in one of these walls and opened it, again without a swipe of his wrist. "This is my house," he said and nodded toward the structure.

Lee took a closer look. It was big, with windows that looked huge, compared to the porthole-like openings that she was used to. There seemed to be two levels, but she couldn't tell how it was divided. "How many accommodation units does it contain?" she asked.

Hardy raised his eyebrows and smiled. "Accommodation units? There are about eight rooms, I guess. Four bedrooms. A living room, my dad's study, my mom's studio and the den."

Lee nodded, even though most of those words didn't mean a thing to her. "And how many families live here?"

"Just one," Hardy said and shut the gate behind her.

Lee stopped and stared. The building was only two levels, but almost as big as her own house, which accommodated fifty families on five levels.

13

Hardy opened the door, again without swiping, just pulling on some kind of handle on one side of the rectangular door that instead of sliding into the wall swung open towards them. Lee stepped inside the house and stared around her. The floor was smooth like she was used to, but there seemed to be walls everywhere, in all possible angles, dividing and arranging the space for different purposes. The smooth floor was covered here and there with some sort of thick fabric in broad, colorful patterns. They were soft and rather comfortable to walk on, once you got used to the idea.

The soles of Lee's feet were sore and aching after the long walk in her flimsy slippers, and she stood for a while letting the softness of the floor covers soothe her weary feet. The inside of Hardy's house was warm and filled with even more unfamiliar smells and sounds. There didn't seem to be anyone around, and Lee breathed a sigh of relief.

Hardy threw his carrying thing on the floor inside the door. Then he walked over to a set of stairs and looked over his shoulder to make sure that Lee was following him. "Come on," he said. "Let's go downstairs. I need to figure out how we're going to do this."

Lee left the soft floor coverings and followed him down a wide staircase into a large, dark space. As Hardy stepped off the bottom step of the stairs, a small light came on and cast a yellow sheen on the surroundings. Hardy kept walking toward a door on the other side of the sparsely furnished room. Lee tried to make sense of the things that she walked past, but most of them were unfamiliar.

Hardy held the door open for her to pass and then shut it behind him. The room they had entered was as big as Lee's accommodation unit back in the dome and seemed to be located mostly underground, judging from the fact that all the windows were up under the ceiling. There wasn't much light coming from the windows, because of plants that were growing right outside.

Hardy indicated with his hand that she should sit down on the sofa that was the first familiar thing Lee had seen in this strange world. Lee sat down, relieved to finally recognize something, but then she yelped with surprise when the piece of furniture seemed to want to swallow her whole.

Hardy sat down next to her and didn't seem to mind the softness of the sofa. Lee grabbed hold of the armrest and pulled herself upright. Shifting a little, she managed to sit up and look around.

"So, what are we going to do now?" Hardy asked. "What is the plan?"

Lee looked at him. He looked worried, and not as in control as he had done by the creek. It bothered him that she was here. She didn't know how she knew that, but she did. "Your dad," she said. "I want to know what he knows about the domes. When we are getting out. If there is something I should be doing to prepare for the move."

Hardy frowned. "The thing is ... I don't know what he would do if I introduced you to him." He leaned forward and put his head in his hands. "I've never even heard of anyone leaving a dome, ever. I never thought about it, but now that I do ... I don't know what would happen. If it is allowed, even."

Lee sighed. "But I'm here. What is the worst thing they can do? Send me back? Well, I want to go back, so fine."

Hardy got up. "I'll go upstairs and try and ask him some questions," he said and walked toward the door. "You wait here. It's probably best if you stay out of sight."

Lee flew up. "No. I want to speak to him." As scary as the thought was, she didn't want to miss her chance of seeing a dad. "I want to hear what he has to say."

Hardy stopped with his hand on the door. "I don't think that is a good idea."

Lee walked over to him. "Please?" she pulled the fabric forward over her hair once more. "Do you think he will be able to tell that I'm … one of them?"

Hardy nodded. "I'm afraid it's pretty obvious, up close," he said.

Lee didn't want to stay in that strange room all alone. "Please?"

"All right." Hardy sighed. "You can come upstairs. But keep your voice down, okay? I have an idea."

Lee followed him up the stairs to the hallway and then up another set of stairs to the second level of the dwelling. There was a smaller, more narrow hallway with doors in every direction, most of them open or at least ajar. Hardy waved at her to come closer, pulled her behind one of the doors and put his finger to her lips as a signal to her to be quiet. Then he moved into the room, knocking on the doorpost as he did so.

"Hey, Dad?" he said, and Lee could hear some movement from inside the room.

"Hardy! You're back! How was your hike?"

Lee moved closer to the wall and peeked through the narrow gap between the wall and the door she was standing behind. She could only see a small fraction of the room inside, but the voice of the person Hardy had spoken to sounded like nothing she had ever heard before, dark and booming. She wished she could see what he looked like, but was afraid to be seen.

"Fine ..." Hardy said, hesitantly. "I saw a fox."

"Did you? Did you get any pictures?"

"No. Something startled it, and it ran away before I got a chance."

Lee pressed closer to the wall, holding her breath, waiting to hear what Hardy would do. Would he reveal her hiding place? Tell his dad that he had someone from the dome in the house?

"Too bad," said the dad-person.

"Yeah …" said Hardy and Lee could hear some sort of tension in his voice. "But Dad, I was wondering …"

There was a soft rustling noise that Lee realized came from the strange clothes that these people wore. The dad-person must have moved. "What, son?"

"The dome …"

Another rustling noise. "What about it?"

"I was wondering … The people who live there …"

"What about them?"

There was silence for a while, and Lee held her breath.

"Do they ever get to come out?"

"Oh, no, son! Never, ever. The inhabs must stay inside the dome. It would kill them to come outside."

14

Lee felt her lungs bursting with a held-in breath but couldn't let it out.

"What do you mean, kill them?" Hardy sounded worried.

"The dome is a completely sterile environment. The inhabs have lived inside that bubble their entire lives, in that perfect world, where there are no diseases or harmful substances. They have no immune system, nothing that would protect them from a simple bug. A cold would kill them."

The room went quiet. Lee pressed her eyes closed, trying to make sense of the unfamiliar words. What did he mean when he said a cold? Cold was a temperature, not a thing. And what was a disease?

"So, what?" Hardy said, and Lee thought it sounded as if his voice was trembling. "If someone left the dome for, like, a few hours, and then went back in? Would they still die?"

The dad-person was quiet for a while. "Perhaps not. Not for a few hours. It depends on what they were exposed to, I guess. And once they returned to the dome, the system would pick up any anomalies and make sure that the inhab received antibiotics or antiviral treatment."

"How?" said Hardy. "If they don't have any diseases, why would they have any medicine?"

"Oh, no, the inhabs don't have any medicine. There aren't even any doctors among them. They don't need to worry about things like that. It's all automated, through the food and water dispensing system, and the diagnostic device they all have implanted in their wrist. Every inhab gets exactly the nutrients and treatments that they need at any given time. It really is a perfectly streamlined system."

"So if someone happened to leave a dome, and perhaps catch a cold," Hardy asked, "all they had to do was go back inside the dome and have some dinner, and everything would be fine?"

"Yeah, hypothetically," the dad-person said. "But no one ever leaves the dome. No one ever wants to."

Hardy was quiet for a while. "Why not?"

"Why would they? They've got everything they need, everything planned and mapped out for them; every decision made, not a problem or worry in the world. It really is the perfect existence."

"Why don't we live there then?"

The dad-person made a strange chuckling noise. "No, son. That's not for us. We're needed out here."

"For what? Why us?"

"Well, someone has to run the show. Monitor the system. It wouldn't function on its own, not indefinitely. We're constantly tweaking the software, making updates, improvements. Just this week, I've been working on some faulty lines of code that had caused some inhabs to get the same food, over and over. It took me two days to sort it out."

Lee bit her lip. Her pizza tablets! She had no idea what faulty lines of code meant, but realized that these Outside people must be keeping a close eye on the ones inside the dome. They even knew what she had for dinner. So did they know that she was missing? What did their systems say about the fact that she hadn't had breakfast or lunch, and probably wouldn't be back in time for dinner either?

The dad kept talking. "I had to reboot an entire database of more than five thousand inhabs, and it has taken all day to get it up and running again. Some of the data is still rendering, and those inhabs might not be back in the system properly until sometime next week. We'll sort it out, but that just goes to show you why we programmers need to monitor the domes. There are just too many bugs in the programming still, after more than seven hundred years."

"Yeah ... About that." Hardy paused before continuing. "How did they come to be living in there? Did they volunteer or ...?"

"Well, not exactly. The people that were offered a space in one of the domes were carefully selected from the remains of the population when things started to go sideways. Most of them were homeless and destitute, with little or no education, living in war zones, and had suffered immensely under the old system, since they were incapable of bettering themselves or changing their destiny. The ones that were deemed to be of value to the gene pool and that scored high on the psychological evaluation tests, to see how they would cope with confinement and so on, were offered a place in one of the domes. Considering what life was like back then, I can't imagine that anyone who was offered a spot turned it down."

Hardy sounded strained. Lee wondered if his dad could tell. "So they volunteered to move into a dome, forever?"

"Well," said the dad-person. "Originally the Doming was a temporary measure. A hundred years was the plan, I think, so that the environment would get a chance to sort itself out. They might have been told that their grandchildren would be able to move back outside, into a world that would be a much better place. But the date for the Un-Doming kept being postponed, for various reasons, and now I think that the plans to let the inhabs out has more or less been canceled. It just wouldn't work. The domes have saved humanity from extinction, but it could so easily go wrong again if we upset the delicate balance. There's just so many of them."

"So ... are they just going to stay in there? Forever?"

"You have to understand that these people are incapable of managing their own lives. Their ancestors were unable to do it 700 years ago, and these people are exactly the same. But don't you worry about them, son. They're fine. They're happy. They have everything they need."

Hardy went quiet for a while. "Do they know ... that they're never getting out?"

The dad-person did the strange chuckle thing again. "They don't even know they're shut in, son. They don't know a thing about the rest of the world. And what you don't know about, you don't worry about. And you don't long for it, either.

Go on now, get started on your homework. That was the deal, remember? You're keeping your grades up, or no more hiking!"

"Yes, Dad," said Hardy.

1 5

He came out of the room and closed the door behind him, revealing Lee, who stood with her back against the wall, just staring at him. He waved at her to follow, but she couldn't move. All the strange things that his dad had said were tumbling around in her brain, so many unfamiliar concepts and thoughts that it hurt to try and understand them all at once. Hardy grabbed her arm and pulled her with him across the hallway and down the stairs, back out the door. Only when they had left the house and gone outside the gate, back down the street a bit, did Hardy speak.

"Did you hear what he said?" he asked.

Lee nodded. She hadn't understood half of it, but she had heard it just fine.

"You've got to get back inside that dome," said Hardy. His face was even paler than before, and he seemed to be in a hurry.

"But ..."

"Now, Lee!" He grabbed her by the arm and started walking back the way they had come, constantly checking over his shoulder.

Lee looked around, trying to soak up as much detail as possible of all the things she saw. Once she had gone back inside the Dome, she would never get to see the Outside again. It wasn't the horrible place she had pictured, but at the same time, there was apparently so much to fear, even though she didn't see anything. What was, for instance, a cold? And would she make it back inside the dome before one of them came and killed her?

They more or less ran through the park, went out the gate in the tall fence and kept up a brisk pace on the way back up along the stream. Lee tried to get Hardy to slow down, but he wouldn't listen. He stopped for a drink, but when Lee bent over the creek, he reached out his hand to stop her.

"Perhaps you shouldn't," he said with a worried frown.

Lee sat back on her heels. "But I'm so thirsty," she complained.

"But it's not ..." He went quiet and looked at her intently, scanning her for something. "You shouldn't drink it," he said.

"I have to," Lee said and put her hand on her stomach. "I haven't had anything to eat all day. I won't be able to keep going unless I have some water, at least. Aren't you hungry?"

Hardy shook his head. "Not really. I had a big lunch before I went out into the woods earlier. It's almost dinnertime, but I can't think about food. Not now."

Lee smiled faintly. "I wish I could have had dinner at your accommodation unit," she said, leaning over to drink. She sat up, wiping her mouth. "What flavor food tablets do you have here in the Outside?"

"Food ... tablets?" Hardy shook his head slowly. "We don't have any food tablets."

Lee frowned. "But what do you eat then?"

Hardy shrugged. "You know … Food."

"But you said you didn't have any?" Lee frowned.

Hardy got up from the ground, reaching out his hand to help her get back up. "We eat actual food," he explained. "Not pills." He looked curious. "What type of tablets do you get?"

Lee looked back down the slope they had just come up. "Well, I heard your … dad talking about us getting the same food several days in a row. I thought that was weird. I've been getting pizza for lunch every day this week."

Hardy grinned. "Nice." Then the grin disappeared. "But as a tablet? What is that like?"

Lee tilted her head to one side. "Not bad. It doesn't taste very much, but more than the porridge tablets, anyway."

"Porridge tablets!" Hardy made a face. "Yuk!"

Lee smiled. "I don't know what that means, but I think that's about right."

Hardy looked up at the tree tops, where the sun was just starting to sink out of sight.

It wasn't very late, but surrounded by the tall trees, shutting out the sunlight, it was already starting to get dark. "We need to keep going. You really have to get back."

"But why?"

He looked worried. "You can't be here," he said and started walking again. "It's not safe."

Lee followed him. It was getting harder and harder to walk; the fading light made it difficult to see where she should put her feet and the intense fatigue and hunger made her lose her balance more than once.

A gnarly old root poked up from the ground in the shadow beside a tall tree, and she fell and grazed her knee on a rock so that the jumpsuit ripped open. She cried out and collapsed on the ground staring at the red substance that seeped from the jagged wound. "What is that? What's happening?"

Hardy turned around and came back. "It's okay," he said and fell to his knees next to her. "It's only a scrape." He checked the wound with a worried frown on his face. "It's not too deep. It needs cleaning, but I think we'd better get you back inside the dome. An open wound is an invitation for bacteria."

She stared at him. "What is bacteria?"

He helped her up and pulled her along with him further upstream. "It's … small things that cause diseases."

"And what is … diseases? Your … dad said something about that too." She stopped and struggled to remember what he had said.

Hardy kept going. "It's when something goes wrong inside the body; bacteria or virus invade the system and cause a person to become sick. They might develop a temperature, or an infection, perhaps. There are many different kinds."

"And we don't have any, inside the dome?"

"That's right."

She hurried after him, limping. "So is that what they mean, when they say that we can't live in the Outside? These bacteria? They try to kill us?"

Hardy shrugged. "Normally it's not a problem. The human body is good at fighting off infections. It has a built-in system. But that system needs practice to develop. If a person has never been in contact with a bacteria or a virus—and you haven't—then your body doesn't know how to fight it."

"So what will happen now? Will I die? Because I went into the Outside and tripped and got a cold on my knee?" Lee couldn't help but feel emotional. There was a thick feeling in her throat, and her eyes were stinging uncomfortably. "And in my eyes, I think. There's something wrong with my eyes." The tears started running down her cheeks, leaving shiny lines in the dust that covered her skin after her long hike down and back up along the stream. "What is happening?"

Hardy stopped and looked at her, staring into her eyes. "I can't see anything wrong with your eyes."

"But they're running over with fluids. I can barely see!" complained Lee, wiping her eyes with her hands.

Hardy just stared at her. "Those are just tears," he said slowly. "Haven't you ever cried before?"

Lee shook her head. "What is that? Is it dangerous? Am I going to die?"

Hardy put his hand on her shoulder. "You are *not* going to die. You are going back inside the dome, and you will eat and drink whatever that dispenser thingy gives you. The food and drink will contain the medicine you need to fight off any infection you might have picked up out here. You will be fine. You just need to get back inside the dome, where you belong. Everything will be fine."

"But my eyes! Will I ever be able to see again?"

Hardy squeezed her shoulder. "You're crying because you're upset. It's perfectly normal. I can't believe you haven't ever cried before. As soon as you calm down, the tears will stop."

She hiccupped and stared at him. "Are you sure? This is normal?"

He nodded and started walking again. "Everyone cries. It's perfectly normal. Sometimes it even feels better after a cry."

A cry. A cold. A bacteria. They had so many unfamiliar things here in the Outside. Lee's head was pounding, one side of her face was still feeling hot and itchy for some reason and she was nauseated after going so many hours without food. Her knee was aching, and she was starting to feel cold again, despite the brisk pace and Hardy's soft but strange half-jumpsuit. She wrapped it closer around her. "I'm afraid," she admitted. "I should never have come out here. What if I die? I'm not supposed to die. I'm only ten. I have fifty-three years left to live. What will happen if I die before it's time? What will happen with my duties? Who's going to do my work?"

Hardy glanced at her. "What do you mean, fifty-three years left? You can't possibly know how long you are going to live."

"Of course I do," she said and stumbled again but managed to regain her balance without falling down. "Everyone knows that. Sixty-three is when you die."

The look he gave her was filled with confusion and something else that she couldn't put her finger on. "Right ..." he said and then looked away. "Sure. I know that. I was thinking of something else."

There was something in his voice that made her feel uncomfortable in a way that she had never experienced before. Like maybe he didn't mean what he said. But why would he say something he didn't mean? What would be the point of that?

They arrived at the bend in the stream where they had first met and continued up the slope and in amongst the trees. From here, it was just a short walk back to the dome. Even if Lee hadn't remembered the way, she could catch glimpses of the dome here and there through gaps in the canopy. No way she could have gotten lost.

Soon they came to the tree-line and Hardy stopped just out of sight, in the shadows. The look in his eyes when he looked up at the enormous curving bubble was a mixture of admiration and fear.

"Wow," he said and shook his head. "I've never seen it up close like this. It's huge."

"It needs to be. A hundred thousand people live in there."

He turned and stared at her. "A hundred thousand? Then ... it's actually not that big. You must be packed in like herring."

She frowned. "What is a herring?"

He smiled at her, and she noticed that her eyes had stopped running over. The brisk walk had drained her of her last strengths, and her knee was throbbing with pain. The right side of her face was still burning, and her stomach muscles were contracting over and over in a very uncomfortable way. She had never been this miserable in her life, but at the same time, she felt strangely relieved. Was it because she was so close to the dome? Or was it because of what Hardy had said, that it sometimes feels better after a cry? Either way, it felt better.

16

Over by the rift, work was still in progress, but the sun was beginning to set behind the trees and Lee didn't think it would be long before the workers stopped for the day. At least, she hoped not. She wouldn't be able to stay out here much longer. She really needed to get back to the accommodation unit, eat something and drink her water. Hopefully, whatever those Outside people put in it would keep her from dying. Oh, water. She was going to drink ten glasses, as soon as she got back. The thought of it made her mouth water.

She smiled faintly. "Yesterday morning I wished for something different in my glass for breakfast. I was so tired of drinking water all the time. I actually hoped for something blue or red to drink. Can you imagine?"

Hardy looked at her with a frown. "Do you mean that you only ever get water to drink? Really? You can't even choose what you get to drink?"

"You heard your dad. Everyone gets what they need. Babies get formula and children get milk. But when you're over seven it's just water, until you're a grown-up and get coffee sometimes."

He shook his head. "So you've never had soda? Or a glass of juice?"

"No," she said, trying to picture what those words might taste like. "What is that? Is it blue?"

He smiled. "Perhaps not blue. But drinks can be yellow or red or brown. Even transparent, like water. There are lots of different colors. Some even have bubbles in them."

She smiled back at him. "It sounds nice. I wish I could have tried it. But perhaps it would only have given me a bacteria."

He was still smiling, but there was a glint in his eye that made her think that his eyes might also start running over. "Yeah. Perhaps."

Her legs felt weak, and she sat down on the ground, leaning back against a tree. Hardy sat down next to her. In the shadows among the trees, the temperature was several degrees lower than out in the sun, and the warmth from their brisk walk up through the woods soon left her body. She started to tremble, only a little at first but soon her teeth were chattering, and her whole body was shaking. Hardy put his arm around her and pulled her closer.

"Wh-what are you doing?" she asked and tried to pull away but didn't have any strength left.

"I'm just trying to keep you warm," he said, and when she felt the warmth from his body, she leaned into it and allowed herself to be held. The violent shaking subsided to a light tremor, and she rested her head against his chest. She could hear the sound of his heart beating inside, fast and strong. It felt strange to be this close to someone. She couldn't remember ever being held like this. But the warmth was soothing, and it was more comfortable to lean against his soft sweater than the rough tree trunk. The Outside was so hard. Her knee was throbbing, but there was no more of that red stuff.

"My dad said ..." began Hardy and she lifted her head slightly to see his face. He looked embarrassed. "... that you have implants?"

She leaned back against his chest and pulled up the sleeve on his half-jumpsuit, showing him the dark pattern interspersed with digits and numbers. He put one finger on it and stroked the skin. "Is it a tattoo?"

"What is a tattoo?" she asked.

"A kind of painting on the skin."

She tried to picture that, but couldn't. "I don't know. There's something inside the arm, beneath it. You can feel it if you press here."

She took his hand and pressed his fingers lightly into the flesh of her wrist, knowing he would be able to make out the square edges of whatever was in there.

"And what are those digits and numbers?"

She turned her arm and looked at it. "That's me. X54-52L. Lee Xanthia."

He loosened his grip around her, just long enough to pull out the shooting thing and hold it above her wrist. There was a brief flash, and Lee could see her wrist, id-code and all, appear on the small screen. Hardy touched the screen and entered her name. "Lee Xanthia. That's a pretty name. Did your mothers name you after someone special?"

Lee frowned. "My mothers didn't name me. The Reproductive and Placement Services did, before they assigned me to them."

He nodded. "You said that, before. You're getting a sister, right?

"Today."

"And you just found out?"

She nodded against his chest. "They called ... yesterday. Strange. It feels like such a long time ago." She was shaking harder now, and her voice sounded weak.

Hardy rubbed her arm to keep her warm. "A lot has happened."

Lee pulled her legs up and wrapped her arms around them. The tear in her jumpsuit was ugly, and her knee was red and sore. "A lot," she agreed, but then her teeth were chattering so hard that it was getting difficult to speak.

She glanced over at the dome where it sounded as if the workers were coming down off the scaffolding. As the sun set, the workers packed up their equipment and returned to their accommodation units. Everything went quiet, but Hardy and Lee sat there a while longer, just to be safe.

When darkness fell, Hardy helped her get up. Her legs were trembling, and it was difficult to walk. He kept his arm around her across the grass over to the gap in the dome. She was shivering and feeling clammy and damp all over. When they came up to the rift, she pulled the fabric off her head, unzipped his strange half-jumpsuit and handed the garment to him. "Thank you," she said. "For ... today. For everything. For telling me things. For not telling your dad. For keeping me warm."

Hardy looked worried. "Are you going to be all right? Will you get into trouble for this? Going outside?"

She shrugged. "I don't know. As far as I know, this has never happened before. And your dad said something about some data being offline. Maybe no one noticed that I was gone? I guess I'll find out."

He nodded. "Take care. And drink lots of water until you start feeling better. Eat everything that dispenser thingy gives you. It's good for you; you know that now."

She smiled, pulled the plastic tarp to the side and stepped through it. "I know a lot now, thanks to you." She raised her hand and waved.

He waved back, turned and hurried back toward the trees. It was quickly becoming dark, but she saw him pull that shooting thing out of his pocket and use it to light his way through the shadows. The light shone on the tree trunks and branches, creating a strange sheen that moved through the darkness for a short while. And then it was gone.

17

There was no one around when Lee emerged from under the scaffolding. It was dinner time, and everyone was in their accommodation units, with their families. She stumbled across the street on sore feet and into the building where she lived, slowly making her way up the stairs. She had never been so happy to see that beige door, exactly like every other door in the entire dome apart from the small number plaque. She raised her hand, and the door slid open.

Her mothers were in the living room, sitting on the sofa. On the floor next to it was a small plastic bassinet on wheels. Through the transparent sides, Lee could see a small bundle, lying perfectly still. She looked over at her mothers. Liesl looked stunned, her mouth opening and closing without making any sound. After an initial pause, Kate flew up and hurried over to her.

"Where have you been?" she said firmly. "What have you done?" She stopped, took a step back and stared at Lee, dirty and disheveled, with a tear in her jumpsuit, shivering and limping. "What happened to you? What in the entire dome has happened to you?"

Lee didn't answer. She just teetered over to the dispensing unit, leaned against the wall and placed her wrist against she scanner. Instead of the usual rattle, the machine stayed silent. That had never happened before. What if the scanning had revealed something inside of her that the dispenser couldn't handle? What would happen then? Would it trigger an alarm, somewhere? Would someone come and take her away, like they had done with the grandmothers when their time had come? Just as Lee was about to collapse on the floor, the machine started working again, but the sound it made was not the usual rattle. Instead, there was a dull thud behind the plastic door.

She pulled her glass from the holder with trembling fingers and placed it in the drinks unit, scanning her wrist once again. Again, there was a delay. The display showed that her wrist had been scanned, but it took a while before the glass started to fill. Lee clung to the wall while she retrieved her food packet, which was much larger than usual. When she grabbed her glass, it was warm and didn't contain water. For some reason that made her eyes run over again. She had gotten her wish, but it had almost cost her her life.

She turned and staggered over to a chair, almost fell into it and took a big gulp of her beverage before tearing open the packet. There were no pills inside. Instead, there was a large, round, soft disc-shaped object with an intense smell and a slightly crumbly texture. She nibbled at it. It was sweet, and a little bit warm, and she immediately took a large bite and chewed eagerly. She swallowed the soft substance down with large gulps of the warm and scented beverage that was starting to warm her up from the inside.

"What is that?" Liesl whispered to Kate. "I've never seen food like that. And what is that she's drinking?"

Lee looked up and saw concern and perhaps even fear on their faces. "It's okay," she said. "Don't worry. I'm going to be fine."

"Don't worry?" Kate said and sat down across from Lee. "Of course we worry when our only child simply disappears. We didn't know what to think. There was no notification from either of our counselors or any message from the authorities. We thought that it might have something to do with the arrival of the new baby, but we weren't sure what we were supposed to do. There were no instructions. It was most disturbing. Where have you been?"

Lee looked at them. She had been gone all day, from dawn to after sundown, and her mothers must have been concerned. Perhaps even frightened. But they had done nothing. They had not looked for her, not contacted the authorities. "Did you tell Helenifer that I was gone?"

Liesl looked at Kate. "I told you we should have contacted her counselor."

Kate shook her head. "And I said no. Do you honestly think that they would give a baby to a set of parents who have misplaced the child they already have?"

Lee leaned back against the backrest and felt the food and drink start to soothe her aches and pains. And her worries too. Perhaps it was just that she was back in her familiar surroundings, but her muscles were slowly relaxing, and the trembling was subsiding. All the frightening thoughts she had experienced out there, in the Outside, crept away into some dark corner of her mind and soon she could hardly remember what it had been that had scared her so.

"Are you going to tell us where you've been?" Kate said, sternly.

Lee smiled. "You wouldn't believe me." She finished the food, down to the last crumb. It had been an amazing experience, eating something with such texture and flavor, but she strongly suspected that tomorrow there would be pills in a small packet again. She took another gulp of the warm, thick beverage and rolled it around her tongue before swallowing. "Did you have your dinner?" she asked.

Liesl shook her head. "No, of course not. I've been so worried; I haven't eaten a thing all day."

Lee looked at Kate who also shook her head.

"We didn't know what to do," she said, and the frown line on her forehead was even more pronounced than usual.

Perhaps there was something in the food and drink that helped with worries as well? Because Lee didn't feel the least bit worried, not anymore. And for every gulp she took of the warm drink, she felt calmer.

"You need to have your dinner," she said and was surprised at how strange her voice sounded. Almost like another person's. And her thoughts didn't feel like her own either. Her experiences from earlier today already felt as if they had happened to someone else.

I'm going to forget it all, she thought and sat up. There was only a little left in her glass, and she desperately wanted to finish it, but there was something inside of her that was clinging to the memories, the insights, the questions that the day's activities had awoken in her. Please don't let me forget, she thought and staggered into her room, leaning against the walls to keep from falling over. She shuffled over to her bed, pulling her jumpsuit off as she went. There was a chute in the wall for used jumpsuits. Usually, they were supposed to wear them for three days, but Lee knew that she would never be able to put on the dirty and torn garment again and dropped it down the chute. She pulled herself up the steps to her bed, suddenly overwhelmed with fatigue. There was someone at the door. She didn't turn her head but knew that her mothers were standing there, staring at her, worried, wondering what was the right thing to do.

"Have your dinner," she slurred at them, without turning her head. "It will make every-thing okay. I'm going to sleep now."

"All right," said Liesl but it didn't sound as if she meant it. "We'll talk about it in the morning."

But we won't, Lee thought. In the morning all of this will be gone. It will be as if it never happened. I will have forgotten everything. Even Hardy.

She clung to the memories of all the strange things she had encountered today, that boy and the furry creature, the water flowing freely in the stream and the houses where the Outsiders lived. The large spaces they occupied and the wide blue sky over their heads all the time. She curled up into a ball and felt a sting on her knee. Her movement had pulled open the wound that had begun to heal. The red stuff was seeping out again. She didn't know what it was called, but she knew that it was okay. Hardy had told her it was fine. It would be fine. The food and drink would make it all go away. And Hardy too.

She touched her finger to the red stuff and looked at it. Then she put her finger against the inside of her bedframe and made a line there. And another. And another. H for Hardy. Perhaps it would help her remember. Remember him. Remember the Outside.

Perhaps not.

THE END!

Thank you for reading!

Would you like to find out what
happened next? Check out the
Dome Series page on my website
www.sandrarandersson.com
for info on the next book in the series,

If you have any questions or comments, you can get in
touch with me via the website listed above or on

www.facebook.com/AuthorSandraR